D0362401

Hello, Family Members,

Learning to read is one of the most i[illegible]s of early childhood. **Hello Reader!** b[illegible]o children become skilled readers who like to read. [illegible]g readers learn to read by remembering frequently used words like "the," "is," and "and"; by using phonics skills to decode new words; and by interpreting picture and text clues. These books provide both the stories children enjoy and the structure they need to read fluently and independently. Here are suggestions for helping your child *before*, *during*, and *after* reading:

Before

- Look at the cover and pictures and have your child predict what the story is about.
- Read the story to your child.
- Encourage your child to chime in with familiar words and phrases.
- Echo read with your child by reading a line first and having your child read it after you do.

During

- Have your child think about a word he or she does not recognize right away. Provide hints such as "Let's see if we know the sounds" and "Have we read other words like this one?"
- Encourage your child to use phonics skills to sound out new words.
- Provide the word for your child when more assistance is needed so that he or she does not struggle and the experience of reading with you is a positive one.
- Encourage your child to have fun by reading with a lot of expression . . . like an actor!

After

- Have your child keep lists of interesting and favorite words.
- Encourage your child to read the books over and over again. Have him or her read to brothers, sisters, grandparents, and even teddy bears. Repeated readings develop confidence in young readers.
- Talk about the stories. Ask and answer questions. Share ideas about the funniest and most interesting characters and events in the stories.

I do hope that you and your child enjoy this book.

—Francie Alexander
Reading Specialist,
Scholastic's Learning Ventures

For Erin Claire, who shines like a star.
— J. Marzollo

For Ruth and Bill, who add sparkle to my life.
— J. Moffatt

Go to www.scholastic.com for Web site information
on Scholastic authors and illustrators.

No part of this publication may be reproduced, or stored in a retrieval system, or transmitted
in any form or by any means, electronic, mechanical, photocopying, recording, or otherwise,
without written permission of the publisher. For information regarding permission, write to
Scholastic Inc., Attention: Permissions Department, 555 Broadway, New York, NY 10012.

ISBN 0-439-11320-2

Text copyright © 2000 by Jean Marzollo.
Illustrations copyright © 2000 by Judith Moffatt.
All rights reserved. Published by Scholastic Inc.
SCHOLASTIC, HELLO READER, CARTWHEEL BOOKS, and associated logos
are trademarks and/or registered trademarks of Scholastic Inc.

Library of Congress Cataloging-in-Publication Data

Marzollo, Jean
        I am a star / by Jean Marzollo; illustrated by Judith Moffatt.
                p. cm. — (Hello reader! science — Level 1)
        Summary: Introduces stars and how they appear in the night sky.
        ISBN 0-439-11320-2 (pbk.)
                1. Stars — Juvenile literature. [1. Stars.] I. Moffatt, Judith, ill. II. Title. III. Series
QB801.7.M386 2000
523.8 — dc21   99-046436

10 9 8 7 6 5 4 3 2 1   00 01 02 03 04

Printed in the U.S.A.   24
First printing, November 2000

I Am a Star

by Jean Marzollo
Illustrated by Judith Moffatt

Hello Reader! Science—Level 1

SCHOLASTIC INC. Cartwheel BOOKS®
New York   Toronto   London   Auckland   Sydney
Mexico City   New Delhi   Hong Kong

I am a star.

You can't see me
in the daytime.
There is too much light.

You can't see me
on a cloudy night.
I hide behind clouds.

You can see stars
on a clear night.
Long ago, people
saw pictures in stars.

The pictures are
called constellations
[con-stel-A-shuns].

Some people saw bears.
Some people saw dippers.

I am the last star
in the Little Dipper's handle.
Can you find me?
I am the North Star.
I am also called Polaris.

Wait a few months.
Look again.

All the stars have moved
except me!
Can you still see me?

I stay in the North.
Sailors use me
to find their way.

The sun is a star.
It is the star nearest to you.
It gives you heat and light.

The moon is not a star.
It reflects the light
of the sun.

To see stars better,
you need a telescope.

The study of stars
is called astronomy
[as-TRON-o-mee].
People who study stars
are called astronomers.
They use BIG telescopes.

How many ways
can you make a star?

USA

China

Israel

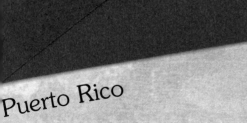

Puerto Rico

Some flags have stars.

Do you know a song about a star?

When you wish upon a star, what do you wish for?